THERE WAS MAGIC INSIDE

THERE WAS MAGIC INSIDE

— DAVID GALCHUTT —

SIMON & SCHUSTER BOOKS FOR YOUNG READERS
Published by Simon & Schuster
New York London Toronto Sydney Tokyo Singapore

A long time ago, in a land far away, there lived a young fisherman named Toshi. Every day Toshi would leave the village of Katsui and walk to the sea with his fishing pole and basket to try to catch fish for his dinner.

Every day he would watch the birds fly overhead and the waves crash against the rocks. And every day he would dream that he was a rich prince instead of a poor fisherman.

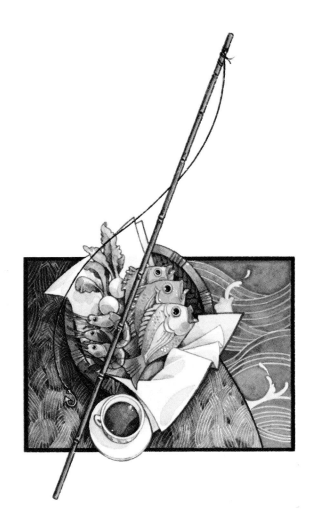

One day as he was fishing and watching and dreaming,
he felt a pull on his line. "A big fish!" he thought,
as he reeled in his catch. But it wasn't a fish, it was
a box—a big box.

There were drawings all over the box, and even
though the box had been tossed about in the sea, the
drawings were still brightly colored.

Toshi put on the cape and the belt and the hat with the bells. He pretended he was a rich prince. Then he sat down and opened the book. "I may not understand the words," thought Toshi, "but I think I understand the pictures."

The first picture showed a man juggling four balls, just like the balls that Toshi had found in the box. Toshi decided to try to juggle, too.

Kersplash! Kerplunk! Kerplank! Kersplosh! The balls fell into the sea.

Toshi watched the balls float away. "Magic may not be as easy as it looks," Toshi thought.

Quickly, Toshi pried open the lid. Inside he found a hat with bells, a cape and a belt, four small balls made of wood, a stick with a laughing jester's head, and a book. "It looks like magic!" Toshi thought.

Suddenly, there was a loud roar from beneath the sea, and a great flame blew across the island.

"Beware! Beware!" called the wise old emperor of Katsui from high atop the village tower. "Xanchi, the sleeping dragon of the sea, has been awakened. Run! Hide! Xanchi, the dreaded dragon, is heading straight for our village!"

Xanchi was a very big dragon. And Xanchi was a very angry dragon. He had been awakened when four wooden balls had hit him on the head, and he was going to find the person who was responsible.

He held the four balls in one claw, and he roared his way across the island.

When Toshi saw Xanchi with the balls, he realized that *he* was responsible for awakening the dragon. He knew he must do something to try to save his village—and he must do it quickly.

"Hurry! Hurry! Xanchi approaches!" the emperor cried. Toshi saw the dragon coming closer. Over the shouts and screams of the fleeing villagers, Toshi heard the dragon's terrible roar and saw his terrible flames. Suddenly, Toshi knew what he would do—he would use magic!

"A wall! We need a wall to keep out the dragon!" Toshi called. He pointed the stick with the laughing jester's head at some tree branches. Nothing happened. Quickly, Toshi looked at the pictures in the book and acted them out. Then he made up a magic spell of his own: "Ribble-rabble. Rigor-rall. Make for me a wall that's tall!"

Magically, a tall wall appeared. But instead of stone, the wall was made of paper.

"They think *that* can stop *me?*" roared Xanchi. With one fiery breath the dragon burned down the wall.

"An army! We need an army to stop the dragon!" Toshi called, as he gathered up some rocks and dewdrops. He pointed the stick with the laughing jester's head at them, but again nothing happened.

So Toshi made up another magic spell: "Bingle-bangle. Blimey-blarmy. I'm calling for a mighty army!"

Suddenly, hundreds of soldiers appeared. "Charge!" shouted Toshi. But the soldiers were stone statues and snowmen, and they could not move.

"They think *those* can stop *me?*" roared the dragon. Xanchi smashed and melted all the soldiers.

The dragon stared at Toshi with blazing red eyes.

Toshi grabbed some flowers, pointed the stick with the laughing jester's head at them, and cried, "Friggidy-quiggidy. Miggidy-mord. Turn into a slaying sword!"

But instead of a sword, the flowers turned into thousands of butterflies.

"They think *those* can stop *me?*" roared the dragon.

Xanchi dropped the four wooden balls so he could fight the butterflies, slashing at them with his great claws. But the butterflies fluttered about the angry dragon like a bright white cloud.

Then Toshi heard a sound never heard before:
a dragon giggle. First a little dragon giggle, then a
louder dragon giggle; then a huge dragon laugh filled
the air. Soon tears of laughter streamed down the
dragon's face.

"Stop! Stop!" pleaded Xanchi. "Oh, please stop! It
tickles so. I can't stand to laugh. It hurts my belly."

The butterflies did not stop.

Stumbling and bumbling, Xanchi backed away as the
butterflies fluttered and tickled. Then, with a giant
guffaw, Xanchi turned away from the village and belly
flopped right back into the sea, where he fell asleep—
exhausted.

All the people of Katsui rejoiced. "Hurray for Toshi! Hurray for Toshi!" They took the young fisherman to the wise old emperor.

"My boy, you have saved the village," the emperor said. "We gratefully honor you."

"But, your excellency," replied Toshi, "I am afraid it was all my fault. I woke the sleeping dragon by accident when I dropped my wooden balls."

"Then all the more reason to honor you," said the emperor, as he took off his royal robe and wrapped it around Toshi. "Your honest confession, your sense of responsibility, and your bravery will be rewarded. From this day on you are Prince of the Dragon and will be part of my royal court."

Toshi bowed humbly to the emperor.

Prince Toshi put the hat with the bells, the cape and the belt, the four wooden balls, the stick with the laughing jester's head, and the book back in the box.

He hoped he would never need them again. But if he did, he knew that when he opened the box he would find there was magic inside!

To my parents, Ron and Cherie

SIMON & SCHUSTER BOOKS FOR YOUNG READERS
Simon & Schuster Building, Rockefeller Center
1230 Avenue of the Americas, New York, New York 10020
Copyright © 1993 by David Galchutt
SIMON & SCHUSTER BOOKS FOR YOUNG READERS
is a trademark of Simon & Schuster.
Designed by Vicki Kalajian
The text of this book was set in Palatino.
The display type is Harlequin.
The illustrations were done in watercolor.
Manufactured in the United States of America

10 9 8 7 6 5 4 3 2 1

Library of Congress Cataloging-in-Publication Data
Galchutt, David. There was magic inside / written and illustrated
by David Galchutt. p. cm. Summary: A fisherman pulls from the sea
a colorful box containing what appear to be magic things,
only to be confronted by a frightening dragon
on which he must test his newfound magic.
[1. Magic—Fiction. 2. Dragons—Fiction.] I. Title. PZ7.G13038Th
1993 [E]—dc20 91-44017 CIP ISBN: 0-671-75978-7